ILLUSTRATED CLASSICS

Pinocchio

AND OTHER CLASSIC TALES

COMPILED BY

PATRICIA MOORE

NEW DELHI (INDIA)

ILLUSTRATED CLASSICS

Pinocchio

AND OTHER CLASSIC TALES

Published by

MG BOOKS

An Imprint of

MAANU GRAPHICS

MAANU GRAPHICS

(PUBLISHERS OF GENERAL BOOKS)

5FF, Ganpati Bhawan, 21 Ansari Road,
Darya Ganj, New Delhi-110002
Ph: 65285220, 64138266
E-mail : maanugraphics@yahoo.com
mgbooks.maanu@yahoo.com

Printed at

Satyam Enterprises, Delhi

CONTENTS

Geppetto created a wooden puppet

PINOCCHIO

One day, Geppetto, who earned his living making puppets for travelling threatres, started to carve a puppet out of a piece of wood from a tree which had blown down in a gale. It was very easy to carve that special piece of wood and, as he happily worked away, he pictured in his mind the sort of son he would like to have.

Miraculously, the puppet he created was the exact image of the son he longed for. Geppetto was amazed. "He looks just like the son of my dreams," he cried. "What lovely, rosy cheeks he has."

Suddenly the puppet seemed to move. That was not possible! But it was. Before Geppetto could stop him, the puppet ran into the street and started jumping over anything that got in his way. People in the street looked on in

Geppetto decided to tighten all his nuts and boltsso that he would not fall apart

astonishment as Geppetto ran after the puppet calling, "Come here, Pinocchio. Do as you are told."

He called the puppet Pinocchio, as that had always been his favourite name. When he caught up with the boy, Geppetto hugged him and called him "son". Then, as Pinocchio seemed to be always moving around, Geppetto decided to tighten all his nuts and bolts so that he would not fall apart. This was not very pleasant for the little one and when Geppetto started to tighten the joint in his neck, he called out, "Be careful, Daddy! You are hurting me."

"It's a miracle!" exclaimed Geppetto. "He speaks just like a real child."

Afterwards, he dressed the boy in smart, red shorts and a blue shirt. He would have to make sure that Pinocchio received a good education so that he would grow up to be successful. The next morning, Geppetto sold his only winter coat so that he could buy all the books and pencils Pinocchio needed to take to school.

"Be a good boy at school," said Geppetto as he kissed the boy goodbye.

On the way to school, Pinocchio met two naughty boys who, on seeing his brand-new books, offered to buy them from him. Pinocchio readily agreed and, with the money, he bought a ticket to see a show at a nearby theatre.

The show began. Several puppets dressed in a variety of costumes came on stage and danced. In his enthusiasm Pinocchio leaped up to join them and started dancing too. The audience loved it and clapped widly, showering him with coins.

Noting how popular he was, the owner of the theatre gave Pinocchio three gold coins on condition that he performed every day. Geppetto would be very disappointed if he knew what Pinocchio was doing. The boy was not turning out as he had hoped. Worse was to follow because, after leaving the theatre, Pinocchio did not go home. Instead he wandered around, marvelling at all the sights but soon night began to fall.

Suddenly, two scoundrels, a fox who passed himself off as a cripple and a cat who pretened to be blind, approached the puppet and started to ask him questions. Pinocchio

The two villains entertained Pinocchio with a dinner

boasted that he was a dancer in the theatre and that he had three gold coins. He even showed them the money so they would not think he was making it up.

The two rascals continued talking to Pinocchio and soon they had convinced him not to trust the theatre owner, saying that they knew him well and, that although he had been generous that day in order to gain Pinocchio's confidence, he would soon stop paying him.

"Come with us," said the fox. "You'll not only have a good time but we'll make you rich as well."

"And famous," added the cat. They even invited him to dinner.

Pinocchio willingly followed the two rogues. The dinner was splendid but when it was finished the two villains cunningly escaped through a window and left poor Pinocchio to pay for the banquet with one of his gold coins. He had had the first important lesson of his life but would he learn from it? Remembering his good father, he decided to return home. The night was very dark so he was a little frightened when he saw two figures approaching.

The Blue Fairy said "I know that you are telling lies"

The figures had blankets over their heads with small holes cut at eye level. An owl, who had been snoozing on a branch of a nearby tree, started screeching. The wise owl had guessed what was about to happen and was trying to warn the little puppet. As it feared, the figures robbed him of everything he had.

The hooded figures turned out to be the two rogues who had tricked Pinocchio before. This time they tied him up and left him hanging upside down from the branch of a tree.

Luckily for Pinocchio, the owl took pity on him and, with great difficulty, managed to free him. This was very good of the owl as, normally, owls are shy creatures and keep away from strangers. It then carried Pinocchio to its home in the nearby tree.

The Blue Fairy, who only appeared in times of trouble, was waiting for Pinocchio when he arrived at the owl's home. She began asking him questions but Pinocchio, trying to sound important, answered her with lies. With each lie, his nose grew a little longer until it was enormous. As the Blue Fairy listened to him, she realised that Pinocchio had forgotten all about his father and had not

"Hurry up", said the street urchin

even considered how worried he would be.

She interrupted the puppet.

"I know that you are telling lies," she said angrily. "I can see everything and know everything. At this very moment your good father is risking his life searching for you along the cliffs."

At last, Pinocchio realised the error of his ways and promised that he would be good in future. He even cried a little.

The fairy forgave him and, with a sweep of her wand, she changed his nose back to its proper size. She told him to go at once in search of Geppetto andhe promised to do just that. The owl and the other birds showed their delight by chirping merrily. But did Pinocchio really mean what he said?

He did at the time but all his good intentions came to nothing when he was spotted by a street urchin. Pinocchio refused to go along with him but inthe end he had no choice.

"Hurry up", said the street urchin. "The stagecoach to Fun City will be passing soon. You will really enjoy it there."

Pinocchio jumped into a boat

When the stagecoach arrived it was full of naughty, lazy boys and with much pushing Pinocchio and his new friend managed to climb aboard.

Pinocchio was astonished when he noticed the ears of some of the boys. They were very, very long. Then to his dismay he realised that his own ears were growing and he was beginning to look like a donkey.

Pinocchio decided that it would be a good idea to escape from a city where little boys turned into donkeys so that unscrupulous men could parade them at fairs for people to make fun of. Luckily for him, as he was trying to escape, his friend, the owl, appeared and saved him.

As they were flying away the owl told Pinocchio that Geppetto had gone out to sea in a boat in search of his new son and that an enormous whale had swallowed him. For the first time Pinocchio realised just how badly he had behaved towards his father and how much he loved him. Eager to save him, Pinocchio jumped into a boat.

How difficult it was to make progress as the huge waves threatened to capsize the boat!

Pinocchio threw himself into his father's arms

The sea became more choppy and eventually the fragile boat was engulfed by water. The enormus whale that had swallowed Geppetto was lurking nearby and quickly swallowed Pinocchio as well.

Pinocchio could not believe his eyes for there was Geppetto sitting in his boat. Overjoyed, he threw himself into his father's arms. Realising that Geppetto was very weak, Pinocchio vowed to save him at all costs. Luckily, the light from the boat's lantern enabled him to search for something to help them to escape.

As it swallowed just about everything that got in its way, there were many strange things in the whale's stomach. Pinocchio picked up an oar and tickled the whale's throat with it. This made the monster cough loudly and as it did so Pinocchio grabbed his father and they both shot out of the whale's mouth.

Pinocchio tried to carry Geppetto to the surface but he was too heavy. They were both getting weaker by the minute and Pinocchio was afraid that they were going to drown. Suddenly a dolphin appeared and sent them flying up to the surface and they drifted on to a sandy beach.

Pinocchio and Geppetto were most living that ever lived

Oh, no! His father was not breathing and Pinocchio burst into tears, blaming himself for his death. But help was at hand for, at that moment, the Blue Fairy came flying through the air and, smiling at the little puppet, touched the old man with her magic wand. Geppetto opened his eyes and so the great love he had for his son was rewarded.

After restoring Geppetto to life the Blue Fairy touched the puppet with her magic wand and changed him into a real, live boy. Now the good man really had a proper son, the most loving that ever lived.

"The Emperor is in the Wardrobe"

THE EMPEROR'S NEW CLOTHES

Many years ago there lived an Emperor who was so fond of new clothes that he spent all his money on them in order to be beautifully dressed. He did not care about his soldiers, he did not care about the theater; he only liked to go out walking to show off his new clothes. He had a coat for every hour of the day; and just as they say of a King, "He is in the council-chamber," here they always said, "The Emperor is in the wardrobe."

In the great city in which he lived there was always something going on; every day many strangers came there. One day two impostors arrived who gave themselves out as weavers, and said that they knew how to manufacture the most beautiful cloth imaginable. Not only were the texture and

"This Cloth Must Be Woven"

pattern uncommonly beautiful, but the clothes which were made of the stuff possessed this wonderful property: they were invisible to anyone who was not fit for his office, or who was unpardonably stupid.

"Those must indeed be splendid clothes," thought the Emperor. "If I had them on I could find out which men in my kingdom are unfit for the offices they hold; I could distinguish the wise from the stupid! Yes, this cloth must be woven for me at once." And he gave both the impostors much money, so that they might begin their work.

They placed two weaving-looms, and began to do as if they were working, but they had not the least thing on the looms. They also demanded the finest silk and the best gold, which they put in their pockets, and "worked" at the empty looms till late into the night.

"I should like very much to know how far they have got on with the cloth," thought the Emperor. But at once he remembered that whoever was stupid or not fit for his office would not be able to see it.

Now he certainly believed that he had nothing to fear for himself, but he wanted first

"Lovely, Most Lovely!"

to send somebody else in order to see how he stood with regard to his office. Everybody in the whole town knew what a wonderful power the cloth had, and they were all curious to see how bad or how stupid their neighbor was.

"I will send my old and honored minister to the weavers," thought the Emperor. "He can judge best what the cloth is like, for he has intellect, and no one understands his office better than he."

Now the good old minister went into the hall where the two impostors sat drinking at the empty weaving-looms. "Dear me!" thought the old minister, opening his eyes wide, "I can see nothing!" But he did not say so.

Both the impostors begged him to be so kind as to step closer, and asked him if it were not a beautiful texture and lovely colors. They pointed to the empty loom, and the poor old minister went forward rubbing his eyes; but he could see nothing, for there was nothing there.

"Dear, dear!" thought he, "Can I be stupid? I have never thought that, and nobody must know it! Can I be not fit for my office? No, I must certainly not say that I cannot see the cloth!"

"Have you nothing to say about it?" asked one of the men who was weaving.

"Oh, it is lovely, most lovely!" answered the old minister, looking through his spectacles. "What a texture! What colors! Yes, I will tell the Emperor that it pleases me very much."

"Now we are delighted at that," said both the weavers, and they named the colors and explained the make of the texture.

The old minister paid great attention, so that he could tell the same to the Emperor when he came back to him, which he did.

The impostors now wanted more money, more silk, and more gold to use in their weaving. They put it all in their own pockets, and there came no threads on the loom, but they went on as they had done before at the empty loom.

The Emperor soon sent another worthy statesman to see how the weaving was getting on, and whether the cloth would soon be finished. It was the same with him as the first one; he looked and looked, but because there was nothing on the empty loom he could see nothing.

"Is it not a beautiful piece of cloth?" asked the two impostors, and they pointed to and described the splendid material which was not there.

"Stupid I am not!" thought the man, "so it must be my good office for which I am not fitted. It is strange, certainly, but no one must be allowed to notice it." And so he praised the cloth which he did not see, and expressed to them his delight at the beautiful colors and the splendid texture. "Yes, it is quite beautiful," he said to the Emperor.

Everybody in the town was talking of the magnificent cloth.

Now the Emperor wanted to see it himself while it was still on the loom. With a great crowd of select followers, amongst whom were both the worthy statesmen who had already been there before, he went to the cunning impostors, who were now weaving with all their might, but without fiber or thread.

"Stupid I Am Not!"

"Is it not splendid!" said both the old statesmen who had already been there. "See, your Majesty, what a texture! What colors!" And then they pointed to the empty loom, for they believed that the others could see the cloth quite well.

"What!" thought the Emperor, "I can see nothing. This is indeed horrible! Am I stupid? Am I not fit to be Emperor? That is the most dreadful thing that could happen to me.

"Oh, it is very beautiful," he said out loud. "It has my gracious approval." And then he nodded pleasantly, and examined the empty loom, for he would not say that he could see nothing.

His whole court round him looked and looked, and saw no more than the others; but they said, like the Emperor, "Oh! It is beautiful!" And they advised him to wear these new and magnificent clothes for the first time at the great procession which was soon to take place. "Splendid! Lovely! Most beautiful!" went from mouth to mouth; everyone seemed delighted over them, and the Emperor gave to the impostors the title of Court Weavers to the Emperor.

Needles Without Thread

Throughout the whole of the night before the morning on which the procession was to take place, the impostors were up and were working by the light of more than sixteen candles. The people could see that they were very busy making the Emperor's new clothes ready. They pretended they were taking the cloth from the loom, cut with huge scissors in the air, sewed with needles without thread, and then said at last, "Now the clothes are finished!"

The Emperor came himself with his most distinguished knights, and each impostor held up his arm just as if he were holding something, and said, "See! Here are the breeches! Here is the coat! Here the cloak!" and so on.

"Spun clothes are so comfortable that one would imagine one had nothing on at all; but that is the beauty of it!" said all the knights, but they could see nothing, for there was nothing there.

"Will it please your Majesty graciously to take off your clothes," said the impostors, "then we will put on the new clothes, here before the mirror."

"What Material! What Colors!"

The Emperor took off all his clothes, and the impostors placed themselves before him as if they were putting on each part of his new clothes as was ready, and the Emperor turned and bent himself in front of the mirror.

"How beautifully they fit! How well they sit!" said everybody. "What material! What colors! It is a gorgeous suit!"

"They are waiting outside with the canopy which your Majesty is to have borne over you in the procession," announced the Master of the Ceremonies.

"Look, I am ready," said the Emperor. "Doesn't it sit well!" And he turned himself again to the mirror to see if his finery was on all right.

The chamberlains who were used to carry the train put their hands near the floor as if they were lifting up the train; then they did as if they were holding something in the air. They would not have it noticed that they could see nothing.

So the Emperor went along in the procession under the splendid canopy, and all the people in the streets and at the windows

"But He Has Nothing On!"

said, "How matchless are the Emperor's new clothes! That train fastened to his dress, how beautifully it hangs."

No one wished it to be noticed that he could see nothing, for then he would have been unfit for his office, or else very stupid. None of the Emperor's clothes had met with such approval as these had.

"But he has nothing on!" said a little child at last.

"Just listen to the innocent child!" said the father, and each one whispered to his neighbor what the child had said.

"But he has nothing on!" the whole of the people called out at last.

This struck the Emperor, for it seemed to him as if they were right; but he thought to himself, "I must go on with the procession now." And the chamberlains walked along still more uprightly, holding up the train which was not there at all!

The Rock was Called Ahtola

THE SEA KING'S GIFT

There was once a fisherman who was called Matte. He lived by the shore of the big sea; where else could he live? He had a wife called Maie; could you find a better name for her? In winter they dwelt in a little cottage by the shore, but in spring they flitted to a red rock out in the sea and stayed there the whole summer until it was autumn. The cottage on the rock was even smaller than the other; it had a wooden bolt instead of an iron 3ock to the door, a stone hearth, a flagstaff, and a weathercock on the roof.

The rock was called Ahtola, and was not larger than the market-place of a town. Between the crevices there grew *a* little rowan tree and four alder bushes. Heaven only knows how they ever came there; perhaps they were brought by the winter storms.

Salmon, Herring, and Cod

Besides that, there flourished some tufts of velvety grass, some scattered reeds, two plants of the yellow herb called tansy, four of a red flower, and a pretty white one; but the treasures of the rock consisted of three roots of garlic, which Maie had put in a cleft.

Rock walls sheltered them on the north side, and the sun shone on them on the south. This does not seem much, but it sufficed Maie for a herb plot.

All good things go in threes, so Matte and his wife fished for salmon in spring, for herring in summer, and for cod in winter. When on Saturdays the weather was fine and the wind favorable, they sailed to the nearest town, sold their fish, and went to church on Sunday.

But it often happened that for weeks at a time they were quite alone on the rock Ahtola, and had nothing to look at except their little yellow-brown dog, which bore the grand name of Prince, their grass tufts, their bushes and blooms, the sea bays and fish, a stormy sky, and the blue, white-crested waves. For the rock lay far away from the land, and there were no green islets or human habitations for miles round; only here and there appeared a

The Idea of a Cow

rock of the same red stone as Ahtola, besprinkled day and night with the ocean spray.

Matte and Maie were industrious, hard-working folk, happy and contented in their poor hut, and they thought themselves rich when they were able to salt as many casks of fish as they required for winter and yet have some left over with which to buy tobacco for the old man, and a pound or two of coffee for his wife, with plenty of burned corn and chicory in it.

Besides that, they had bread, butter, fish, a beer cask, and a buttermilk jar; what more did they require? All would have gone well had not Maie been possessed with a secret longing which never let her rest; and this was, how she could manage to become the owner of a cow.

"What would you do with a cow?" asked Matte. "She could not swim so far, and our boat is not large enough to bring her over here; and even if we had her, we have nothing to feed her on."

"We have four alder bushes and sixteen tufts of grass," rejoined Maie.

"Yes, of course," laughed Matte, "and we also have three plants of garlic. Garlic would be fine feeding for her."

"Every cow likes salt herring," rejoined his wife. "Even Prince is fond of fish."

"That may be," said her husband. "Methinks she would soon be a dear cow if we had to feed her on salt herring. All very well for Prince, who fights with the gulls over the last morsel. Put the cow out of your head, mother, we are very well off as we are."

Maie sighed. She knew well that her husband was right, but she could not give up the idea of a cow. The buttermilk no longer tasted as good as usual in the coffee; she thought of sweet cream and fresh butter, and of how there was nothing in the world to be compared with them.

One day as Matte and his wife were cleaning herring on the shore they heard Prince barking, and soon there appeared a gaily painted boat with three young men in it, steering towards the rock. They were students, on a boating excursion, and wanted to get something to eat.

"Bring us a pudding, good mother," cried they to Maie.

"Ah! If only I had such a thing!" sighed Maie.

"A can of fresh milk, then," said the students; "but it must not be skim."

"Yes, if only I had it!" sighed the old woman, still more deeply.

"What! Haven't you got a cow?"

Maie was silent. This question so struck her to the heart that she could not reply. "We have no cow," Matte answered; "but we have good smoked herring, and can cook them in a couple of hours."

"All right, then, that will do," said the students, as they flung themselves down on the rock, while fifty silvery-white herring were turning on the spit in front of the fire.

"What's the name of this little stone in the middle of the ocean?" asked one of them.

"Ahtola," answered the old man.

"Well, you should want for nothing when you live in the Sea King's dominion."

"Bring Us a Pudding!"

Matte did not understand. He had never read about and knew nothing of the sea gods of old, but the students proceeded to explain to him.

"Ahti," said they, "is a mighty king who lives in his dominion of Ahtola, and has a rock at the bottom of the sea, and possesses besides a treasury of good things. He rules over all fish and animals of the deep; he has the finest cows and the swiftest horses that ever chewed grass at the bottom of the ocean. He who stands well with Ahti is soon a rich man, but one must beware in dealing with him, for he is very changeful and touchy.

"Even a little stone thrown into the water might offend him, and then as he takes back his gift, he stirs up the sea into a storm and drags the sailors down into the depths. Ahti owns also the fairest maidens, who bear the train of his queen Wellamos, and at the sound of music they comb their long, flowing locks, which glisten in the water."

"Oh!" cried Matte, "Have your worships really seen all that?"

"We have as good as seen it," said the

"He Who Stands Well With Ahti is Soon Rich"

students. "It is all printed in a book, and everything printed is true."

"I'm not so sure of that," said Matte, as he shook his head.

But the herring were now ready, and the students ate enough for six, and gave Prince some cold meat which they happened to have in the boat. Prince sat on his hind legs with delight and mewed like a pussy cat. When all was finished, the students handed Matte a shining silver coin, and allowed him to fill his pipe with a special tobacco.

They then thanked him for his kind hospitality and went on their journey, much regretted by Prince, who sat with a woeful expression and whined on the shore as long as he could see a flip of the boat's white sail in the distance.

Maie had never uttered a word, but thought all the more. She had good ears, and had laid to heart the story about Ahti. "How delightful," thought she to herself, "to possess a fairy cow! How delicious every morning and evening to draw milk from it, and yet have no trouble about the feeding, and to keep a shelf near the window for dishes of milk

He Did Not Fish on Sunday

and puddings! But this will never be my luck."

"What are you thinking of?" asked Matte.

"Nothing," said his wife; but all the time she was pondering over some magic rhymes she had heard in her childhood from an old lame man, which were supposed to bring luck in fishing.

"What if I were to try?" thought she.

Now this was Saturday, and on Saturday evening Matte never set the herring-net, for he did not fish on Sunday. Towards evening, however, his wife said:

"Let us set the herring-net just this once."

"No," said her husband, "it is a Saturday night."

"Last night was so stormy, and we caught so little," urged his wife; "tonight the sea is like a mirror, and with the wind in this direction the herring are drawing towards land."

"But there are streaks in the north-western sky, and Prince was eating grass this evening," said the old man.

So They Rowed Out

"Surely he has not eaten my garlic," exclaimed the old woman.

"No, but there will be rough weather by to-morrow at sunset," rejoined Matte.

"Listen to me," said his wife, "we will set only one net close to the shore, and then we shall be able to finish up our half-filled cask, which will spoil if it stands open so long."

The old man allowed himself to be talked over, and so they rowed out with the net. When they reached the deepest part of the water, she began to hum the words of the magic rhyme, altering the words to suit the longings of her heart:

Oh, Ahti, with the long, long beard,
    Who dwellest in the deep blue sea,
Finest treasures, have I heard,
    And glittering fish belong to thee.
The richest pearls beyond compare
    Are stored up in thy realm below,
And Ocean's cows so sleek and fair
    Feed on the grass in thy green meadow.

King of the waters, far and near,
    I ask not of thy golden store,

Maie Raised Her Voice and Went on

I wish not jewels of pearl to wear,
    Nor silver either, ask I for,
But one is odd and even is two,
    So give me a cow, Sea King so bold,
And in return I'll give to you
    A slice of the moon, and the sun's gold.

"What's that you're humming?" asked the old man.

"Oh, only the words of an old rhyme that keeps running in my head," answered the old woman, and she raised her voice and went on:

Oh, Ahti, with the long, long beard,
    Who dwellest in the deep blue sea
A thousand cows are in thy herd,
    I pray thee give one unto me.

"That's a stupid sort of song," said Matte. "What else should one beg of the Sea King but fish? But such songs are not for Sunday."

His wife pretended not to hear him, and sang and sang the same tune all the time they were on the water. Matte heard nothing more

The Storm Raged in Every Direction

as he sat and rowed the heavy boat, while thinking of his cracked pipe and the fine tobacco. Then they returned to the island, and soon after went to bed.

But neither Matte nor Maie could sleep a wink; the one thought of how he had profaned Sunday, and the other of Ahti's cow.

About midnight the fisherman sat up, and said to his wife:

"Dost thou hear anything?"

"No," said she.

"I think the twirling of the weathercock on the roof bodes ill," said he; "we shall have a storm."

"Oh, it is nothing but your fancy," said his wife.

Matte lay down, but soon rose again.

"The weathercock is squeaking now," said he.

"Just fancy! Go to sleep," said his wife; and the old man tried to.

For the third time he jumped out of bed.

"Ho! How the weathercock is roaring at the pitch of its voice, as if it had a fire inside it! We are going to have a tempest, and must bring in the net."

Both rose. The summer night was as dark as if it had been October, the weathercock creaked, and the storm was raging in every direction. As they went out, the sea lay around them as white as snow, and the spray was dashing right over the fisher-hut.

In all his life Matte had never remembered such a night. To launch the boat and put to sea to rescue the net was a thing not to be thought of. The fisherman and his wife stood aghast on the doorstep, holding on fast by the doorpost, while the foam splashed over their faces.

"Did I not tell thee that there is no luck in Sunday fishing?" said Matte sulkily; and his wife was so frightened that she never even once thought of Ahti's cows.

As there was nothing to be done, they went in. Their eyes were heavy for lack of slumber, and they slept as soundly as if there had not been such a thing as an angry sea roaring furiously around their lonely dwelling. When they awoke, the sun was high in the heavens, the tempest had ceased, and only the swell of the sea rose in silvery heavings against the red rock.

"What can that be?" said the old woman, as she peeped out of the door.

"It looks like a big seal," said Matte.

"As sure as I live, it's a cow!" exclaimed Maie. And certainly it was a cow, a fine red cow, fat and flourishing, and looking as if it had been fed all its days on spinach. It wandered peacefully up and down the shore, and never so much as even looked at the poor little tufts of grass, as if it despised such fare.

Matte could not believe his eyes, but a cow she seemed, and a cow she was found to be; and when the old woman began to milk her, every pitcher and pan was soon filled with the most delicious milk.

The old man troubled his head in vain as to how she came there, and sallied forth to seek for his lost net. He had not proceeded far when he found it cast up on the shore, and so full of fish that not a mesh was visible.

"It's a Cow!"

"It is all very fine to possess a cow," said Matte, as he cleaned the fish; "but what are we going to feed her on?"

"We shall find some means," said his wife; and the cow found the means herself. She went out and cropped the seaweed which grew in great abundance near the shore, and always kept in good condition. Every one, Prince alone excepted, thought she was a clever beast; but Prince barked at her, for he had now got a rival.

From that day the red rock overflowed with milk and puddings, and every net was filled with fish. Matte and Maie grew fat on this fine living, and daily became richer. She churned quantities of butter, and he hired two men to help him in his fishing. The sea lay before him like a big fish tank, out of which he hauled as many as he required; and the cow continued to fend for herself.

In autumn, when Matte and Maie went ashore, the cow went to sea, and in spring, when they returned to the rock, there she stood awaiting them.

"We shall require a better house," said

Maie the following summer; "the old one is too small for ourselves and the men."

"Yes," said Matte. So he built a large cottage, with a real lock to the door, and a store-house for fish as well; and he and his men caught such quantities of fish that they sold tons of salmon, herring, and cod.

"I am quite overworked with so many folk," said Maie; "a girl to help me would not come amiss."

"Get one, then," said her husband; and so they hired a girl.

Then Maie said: "We have too little milk for all these folk. Now that I have a servant, with the same amount of trouble she could look after three cows."

"All right, then," said her husband, somewhat provoked, "you can sing a song to the fairies."

This annoyed Maie, but nevertheless she rowed out to sea on Sunday night and sang as before:

Oh, Ahti, with the long, long beard,

Who dwellest in the deep blue sea,
A thousand cows are in thy herd,
I pray thee give three unto me.

The following morning, instead of one, three cows stood on the island, and they all ate seaweed and fended for themselves like the first one.

"Art thou satisfied now?" said Matte to his wife.

"I should be quite satisfied," said his wife, "if only I had two servants to help, and if I had some finer clothes. Don't you know that I am addressed as Madam?"

"Well, well," said her husband. So Maie got several servants, and clothes fit for a great lady.

"Everything would now be perfect if only we had a little better dwelling for summer. You might build us a two-story house, and fetch soil to make a garden. Then you might make a little arbor up there to let us have a sea-view; and we might have a fiddler to

The Old House is Too Small

fiddle to us of an evening, and a little steamer to take us to church in stormy weather," she declared.

"Anything more?" asked Matte; but he did everything that his wife wished. The rock Ahtola became so grand and Maie so great that all the sea-urchins and herring were lost in wonderment. Even Prince was fed on beefsteaks and cream scones till at last he was as round as a butter jar.

"Are you satisfied now?" asked Matte.

"I should be quite satisfied," said Maie, "if only I had thirty cows. At least that number is required for such a household."

"Go to the fairies," said Matte.

His wife set out in the new steamer and sang to the Sea King. Next morning thirty cows stood on the shore, all finding food for themselves.

"Know'st thou, good man, that we are far too cramped on this wretched rock, and where am I to find room for so many cows?" asked Maie.

"There is nothing to be done but to pump out the sea," replied Matte.

"Rubbish!" said his wife. "Who can pump out the sea?"

"Try with thy new steamer, there is a pump in it."

Maie knew well that her husband was only making fun of her, but still her mind was set upon the same subject. "I never could pump the sea out," thought she, "but perhaps I might fill it up, if I were to make a big dam. I might heap up sand and stones, and make our island as big again."

Maie loaded her boat with stones and went out to sea. The fiddler was with her, and fiddled so finely that Ahti and Wellamos and all the sea's daughters rose to the surface of the water to listen to the music.

"What is that shining so brightly in the waves?" asked Maie.

"That is sea foam glinting in the sunshine," answered the fiddler.

"Throw out the stones," said Maie.

The people in the boat began to throw out the stones, splash, splash, right and left, into the foam. One stone hit the nose of Wellamos's chief lady-in-waiting, another scratched the Sea Queen herself on the cheek, a third plumped close to Ahti's head and tore off half of the Sea King's beard; then there was a commotion in the sea, the waves bubbled and bubbled like boiling water in a pot.

"Whence comes this gust of wind?" said Maie; and as she spoke the sea opened and swallowed up the steamer. Maie sank to the bottom like a stone, but, stretching out her arms and legs, she rose to the surface, where she found the fiddler's fiddle, and used it as a float. At the same moment she saw close beside her the terrible head of Ahti, and he had only half a beard!

"Why did you throw stones at me?" roared the Sea King.

"Oh, your majesty, it was a mistake! Put some bear's grease on your beard and that will soon make it grow again."

"Dame, did I not give you all you asked for – nay, even more?"

"Truly, truly, your majesty. Many thanks for the cows."

All the Sea's Daughters Rose

"Well, where is the gold from the sun and the silver from the moon that you promised me?"

"Ah, your majesty, they have been scattered day and night upon the sea, except when the sky was overcast," answered Maie slyly.

"I'll teach you!" roared the Sea King; and with that he gave the fiddle such a puff that it sent the old woman up like a skyrocket on to her island. There Prince lay, as famished as ever, gnawing the bones of a crow. There sat Matte in his ragged grey jacket, quite alone, on the steps of the old hut, mending a net.

"Heavens, mother," said he, "where are you coming from at such a whirlwind pace, and what makes you in such a dripping condition?"

Maie looked around her amazed, and said, "Where is our two-story house?"

"What house?" asked her husband.

"Our big house, and the flower garden, and the men and the maids, and the thirty beautiful cows, and the steamer, and everything else?"

Another Scratched the Sea Queen Herself

"You are talking nonsense, mother," said he. "The students have quite turned your head, for you sang silly songs last evening while we were rowing, and then you could not sleep till early morning. We had stormy weather during the night, and when it was past I did not wish to waken you, so rowed out alone to rescue the net."

"But I've seen Ahti," rejoined Maie.

"You've been lying in bed, dreaming foolish fancies, mother, and then in your sleep you walked into the water."

"But there is the fiddle," said Maie.

"A fine fiddle! It is only an old stick. No, no, old woman, another time we will be more careful. Good luck never attends fishing on a Sunday."

Maie looked about her at Ahtola; truly it looked the same as it always had. No sign was there of anything of her greatness: not cows nor servants nor casks overflowing with fish of such miraculous abundance that now seemed to exist only in her visions of them.

Matte was lighting his pipe as she gazed at him; as real as the little red light that

"I'll Teach You!"

glowed from it was her remembrance of all that Ahti had given and then taken away. She brushed her eyes with her hand as if to clear her sight, but all she could see was Prince, frolicking on the bare beach as ever he was wont to do; the same tufts of herbs and reeds as ever; and Matte, looking through narrowed but twinkling eyes at her as the wind whistled around the rock and the old weathercock creaked on the roof.

"Ah well," she thought, "even if it was only a dream, how nice it was to have had all that fresh cream!"

And as she gazed, the sea boiled and bubbled as it had when Ahti had appeared. The foam frothed and gleamed, but the light shining on it was only the reflection of the sun as it lowered itself in the sky before disappearing into the sea.

"Spin All Night Till Early Dawn"

RUMPELSTILTSKIN

There was once upon a time a poor miller who had a very beautiful daughter. Now it happened one day that he had an audience with the King, and in order to appear a person of some importance he told him that he had a daughter who could spin straw into gold.

"Now that's a talent worth having," said the King to the miller; "if your daughter is as clever as you say, bring her to my palace tomorrow, and I'll put her to the test."

When the girl was brought to him he led her into a room full of straw, gave her a spinning-wheel and spindle, and said: "Now set to work and spin all night till early dawn, and if by that time you haven't spun the straw into gold you shall die." Then he closed the door behind him and left her alone inside.

"What Will You Give Me?"

So the poor miller's daughter sat down, and didn't know what in the world she was to do. She hadn't the least idea of how to spin straw into gold, and became at last so miserable that she began to cry. Suddenly the door opened, and in stepped a tiny little man and said: "Good-evening, Miss Miller-maid; why are you crying so bitterly?"

"Oh!" answered the girl, "I have to spin straw into gold, and haven't a notion how it's done."

"What will you give me if I spin it for you?" asked the manikin.

"My necklace," replied the girl.

The little man took the necklace, sat himself down at the wheel, and whir, whir, whir, the wheel went round three times, and the bobbin was full. Then he put on another, and whir, whir, whir, the wheel went round three times, and the second too was full; and so it went on till the morning, when all the straw was spun away, and all the bobbins were full of gold.

As soon as the sun rose the King came, and when he perceived the gold he was astonished and delighted, but his heart only

"When You Are a Queen..."

yearned more than ever after the precious metal.

He had the miller's daughter put into another room full of straw, much bigger than the first, and bade her, if she valued her life, spin it all into gold before the following morning.

The girl didn't know what to do, and began to cry; then the door opened as before, and the tiny little man appeared and said: "What'll you give me if I spin the straw into gold for you?"

"The ring from my finger," answered the girl.

The manikin took the ring, and whir! round went the spinning-wheel again, and when morning broke he had spun all the straw into glittering gold.

The King was pleased beyond measure at the sight, but his greed for gold was still not satisfied, and he had the miller's daughter brought into a yet bigger room full of straw, and said: "You must spin all this away in the night; but if you succeed this time you shall become my wife."

A Messenger to Scour the Land

"She's only a miller's daughter, it's true," he thought; "but I could not find a richer wife if I were to search the whole world over."

When the girl was alone the little man appeared for the third time, and said: "What'll you give me if I spin the straw for you once again?"

"I've nothing more to give," answered the girl.

"Then promise me when you are Queen to give me your first child."

"Who knows what may happen before that?" thought the miller's daughter; and besides, she saw no other way out of it, so she promised the manikin what he demanded, and he set to work once more and spun the straw into gold.

When the King came in the morning, and found everything as he had desired, he straightway made her his wife, and the miller's daughter became a Queen.

When a year had passed a beautiful son was born to her, and she thought no more of the little man, till all of a sudden one day he

"Some Demon Has Told You That!"

stepped into her room and said: "Now give me what you promised."

The Queen was in a great state, and offered the little man all the riches in her kingdom if he would only leave her the child.

But the manikin said: "No, a living creature is dearer to me than all the treasures in the world."

Then the Queen began to cry and sob so bitterly that the little man was sorry for her, and said: "I'll give you three days to guess my name, and if you find it out in that time you may keep your child."

Then the Queen pondered the whole night over all the names she had ever heard, and sent a messenger to scour the land, and to pick up far and near any names he should come across. When the little man arrived on the following day she began with Kasper, Melchior, Belshazzar, and all the other names she knew, in a string, but at each one the manikin called out: "That's not my name."

The next day she sent to inquire the names of all the people in the neighborhood, and had a long list of the most uncommon and extraordinary ones for the little man when he made his appearance.

"Is your name, perhaps, Sheepshanks, Cruickshanks, Spindle-shanks?"

But he always replied: "That's not my name."

On the third day the messenger returned and announced: "I have not been able to find any new names, but as I came upon a high hill round the corner of the wood, where the foxes and hares bid each other good night, I saw a little house, and in front of the house burned a fire, and round the fire sprang the most grotesque little man, hopping on one leg and crying:

'Tomorrow I brew, today I bake,
And then the child away I'll take;
For little deems my royal dame
That Rumpelstiltskin is my name!' "

You may imagine the Queen's delight at hearing the name, and when the little man stepped in shortly afterwards and asked: "Now, my lady Queen, what's my name?" she asked first: "Is your name Conrad?"

"No."

"Is your name Harry?"

"No."

"Is your name, perhaps, Rumpelstiltskin?"

"Some demon has told you that, some demon has told you that!" screamed the little man, and in his rage drove his right foot so far into the ground that it sank in up to his waist; then in a passion he seized the left foot with both hands and tore himself apart.

The King, the Queen, and the little Prince lived happily ever after.

"Put It in a Flowerpot"

THUMBELINA

There was once a woman who wanted to have quite a tiny little child, but she did not know where to get one from. So one day she went to an old witch and said to her: "I should so much like to have a tiny little child; can you tell me where I can get one?"

"Oh, we have just got one ready!" said the witch. "Here is a barley-corn for you, but it's not the kind the farmer sows in his field, or feeds the hens with, I can tell you. Put it in a flowerpot, and then you will see something happen."

"Oh, thank you!" said the woman, and gave the witch a shilling, for that was what it cost. Then she went home and planted the barley-corn; immediately there grew out of it a large and beautiful flower, which looked

"A Beautiful Wife for My Son"

like a tulip, but the petals were as tightly closed as if it were still only a bud.

"What a beautiful flower!" exclaimed the woman, and she kissed the red and yellow petals; and as she kissed them the flower burst open. It was a real tulip, such as one can see any day; but in the middle of the blossom, on the green velvety petals, sat a little girl, quite tiny, trim, and pretty. She was scarcely half a thumb in height, so they called her Thumbelina.

An elegant polished walnut-shell served Thumbelina as a cradle, the blue petals of a violet were her mattress, and a rose-leaf her coverlet.

There she lay at night, but in the day-time she used to play about on the table; here the woman had put a bowl, surrounded by a ring of flowers, with their stalks in water, in the middle of which floated a great tulip petal, and on this Thumbelina sat, and sailed from one side of the bowl to the other, rowing herself with two white horse-hairs for oars. It was such a pretty sight! She could sing, too, with a voice more soft and sweet than had ever been heard before.

She Began to Cry Bitterly

One night, when she was lying in her pretty little bed, an old toad crept in through a broken pane in the window. She was very ugly, clumsy, and clammy; she hopped on to the table where Thumbelina lay asleep under the red rose leaf.

"This would make a beautiful wife for my son," said the toad, taking up the walnut-shell with Thumbelina inside, and hopping with it through the window into the garden.

There flowed a great wide stream, with slippery and marshy banks; here the toad lived with her son. Ugh! How clammy he was, just like his mother! "Croak, croak, croak!" was all he could say when he saw the pretty little girl in the walnut-shell.

"Don't talk so loud, or you'll wake her," said the old toad. "She might escape us even now; she is as light as a feather. We will put her at once on a broad water-lily leaf in the stream. That will be quite an island for her, she is so small and light. She can't run away from us there, whilst we are preparing the guest-chamber under the marsh where she shall live."

Away Floated the Leaf

Outside in the brook grew many water-lilies, with broad green leaves, which looked as if they were swimming about on the water. The leaf farthest away was the largest, and to this the old toad swam with Thumbelina in her walnut-shell.

The tiny Thumbelina woke up very early in the morning, and when she saw where she was she began to cry bitterly; for on every side of the great green leaf was water, and she could not get to the land.

The old toad was down under the marsh, decorating her room with rushes and yellow marigold leaves, to make it very grand for her new daughter-in-law; then she swam out with her ugly son to the leaf where Thumbelina lay. She wanted to fetch the pretty cradle to put it into the room before Thumbelina herself came there. The old toad bowed low in the water before her, and said: "Here is my son; you shall marry him, and live in great magnificence down under the marsh."

"Croak, croak, croak!" was all that the son could say. Then they took the neat little cradle and swam away with it; but Thum-belina sat alone on the great green leaf and wept, for she did not want to live with the clammy toad, or marry her ugly son.

The little fishes swimming about under the water had seen the toad quite plainly, and heard what she had said; so they put up their heads to see the little girl. When they saw her, they thought her so pretty that they were very sorry she should go down with the ugly toad to live. "That must not happen," they said amongst themselves.

They assembled in the water round the green stalk which supported the leaf on which she was sitting, and nibbled the stem in two. Away floated the leaf down the stream, bearing Thumbe-lina far beyond the reach of the toad.

On she sailed past several towns, and the little birds sitting in the bushes saw her, and sang, "What a pretty little girl!" The leaf floated farther and farther away; thus Thumbelina left her native land.

A beautiful little white butterfly fluttered above her, and at last settled on the leaf. Thumbelina pleased him, and she, too, was delighted, for now the toads could not reach her, and it was so beautiful where she was travelling; the sun shone on the water and made it sparkle like the brightest silver. She took off her sash, and tied one end round the butterfly; the other end she fastened to the leaf, so that now it glided along with her faster than ever.

A great finch came flying past; he caught sight of Thumbelina, and in a moment he had flown off with her to a tree. The green leaf floated away down the stream, and the butterfly with it, for he was fastened to the leaf and could not get loose from it. Oh, dear! How terrified poor little Thumbelina was when the finch flew off with her to the tree!

But she was especially distressed on the beautiful white butterfly's account, as she had tied him fast, so that if he could not get away he must starve to death. But the finch did not trouble himself about that; he sat down with her on a large green leaf, gave her the honey out of the flowers to eat, and told her that she was very pretty, although she wasn't in the least like a finch.

Later on, all the other finches who lived in the same tree came to pay calls; they

The Finch Flew Off With Her

examined Thumbelina closely, and remarked, "Why, she has two long legs! How very miserable!"

"She has no beak!" cried another.

"How ugly she is!" said all the lady finches — and yet Thumbelina was really very pretty.

The finch who had stolen her knew this very well; but when he heard all the ladies saying she was ugly, he began to think so too, and would not keep her; Thumbelina could go wherever she liked. So he flew down from the tree with her and put her on a daisy. There she sat and wept, because she was so ugly that the finch would have nothing to do with her; and yet she was the most beautiful creature imaginable, so soft and delicate, like the loveliest rose leaf.

The whole summer poor little Thumbelina lived alone in the great wood. She braided a bed for herself of blades of grass, and hung it up under a clover leaf, so that she was protected from the rain; she gathered honey from the flowers for food, and drank the dew on the leaves every morning. Thus the summer and autumn passed, but then came winter — the long, cold winter.

Then Came the Long, Cold Winter

All the birds who had sung so sweetly about her had flown away; the trees shed their leaves; the flowers died; the great clover leaf under which she had lived curled up, and nothing remained of it but the withered stalk. She was terribly cold, for her clothes were ragged, and she herself was so small and thin. Poor little Thumbelina! She would surely be frozen to death.

It began to snow, and every snow-flake that fell on her was to her as a whole shovelful thrown on one of us, for we are so big, and she was only an inch high. She wrapped herself round in a dead leaf, but it was torn in the middle and gave her no warmth; she was trembling with cold.

Just outside the wood where she was now living lay a great corn field. But the corn had been gone a long time; only the dry, bare stubble was left standing in the frozen ground. This made a forest for her to wander about in. All at once she came across the door of a field-mouse, who had a little hole under a corn stalk.

There the mouse lived warm and snug, with a store room full of corn, and a splendid

"You May Spend the Winter with Me"

kitchen and dining room. Poor little Thumbelina went up to the door and begged for a little piece of barley, for she had not had anything to eat for the last two days.

"Poor little creature!" said the field-mouse, for she was a kindhearted old thing at bottom. "Come into my warm room and have some dinner with me."

As Thumbelina pleased her, she said: "As far as I am concerned you may spend the winter with me; but you must keep my room clean and tidy, and tell me stories, for I like that very much."

And Thumbelina did all that the kind old field-mouse asked, and did it remarkably well, too.

"Now I am expecting a visitor," said the field-mouse one day; "my neighbor comes to call on me once a week. He is in better circumstances than I am, has great, big rooms, and wears a fine white velvet coat. If you could only marry him, you would be well provided for. But he is blind. You must tell him all the prettiest stories you know."

But Thumbelina did not trouble her head

Where the Dead Bird Lay

about him, for he was only a mole. He came and paid them a visit in his white velvet coat.

"He is so rich and so accomplished," the field-mouse told her. "His house is twenty times larger than mine; he possesses great knowledge, but he cannot bear the sun and the beautiful flowers and speaks slightingly of them, for he has never seen them."

Thumbelina had to sing to him, so she sang "Ladybird, ladybird, fly away home!" and other songs so prettily that the mole fell in love with her; but he did not say anything, as he was a very cautious man.

A short time before he had dug a long passage through the ground from his own house to that of his neighbor; in this he gave the field-mouse and Thumbelina permission to walk as often as they liked. But he begged them not to be afraid of the dead bird that lay in the passage: it was a real bird with beak and feathers, and must have died a little time ago, and now laid buried just where he had made his tunnel.

The mole took a piece of rotten wood in his mouth, for that glows like fire in the dark, and went in front, lighting them through the

"Farewell, Pretty Little Bird!"

long dark passage. When they came to the place where the dead bird lay, the mole put his broad nose against the ceiling and pushed a hole through, so that the daylight could shine down.

In the middle of the path lay the swallow, his pretty wings pressed close to his sides, his claws and head drawn under his feathers; the poor bird had evidently died of cold. Thumbelina was very sorry, for she was very fond of all little birds; they had sung and twittered so beautifully to her all through the summer.

But the mole kicked him with his bandy legs and said: "Now he can't sing any more! It must be very miserable to be a little bird! I'm thankful that none of my little children are; birds always starve in winter."

"Yes, you speak like a sensible man," said the field-mouse, "what has a bird, in spite of all his singing, in the winter time? He must starve and freeze, and that must not be very pleasant for him, I must say!"

Thumbelina did not say anything; but when the other two had passed on she bent down to the bird, brushed aside the feathers

"Thank You, Pretty Little Child!"

from his head, and kissed his closed eyes gently. "Perhaps it was he that sang to me so prettily in the summer," she thought. "How much pleasure he did give me, dear little bird!"

The mole closed up the hole which let in the light, and he then escorted the ladies home. But Thumbelina could not sleep that night; so she got out of bed, and braided a great big blanket of straw, and carried it off, and spread it over the dead bird, and piled upon it thistle-down as soft as cotton-wool, which she had found in the field-mouse's room, so that the poor little thing should lie warmly buried.

"Farewell, pretty little bird!" she said. "Farewell, and thank you for your beautiful songs in the summer, when the trees were green, and the sun shone down warmly on us!" Then she laid her head against the bird's heart. But the bird was not dead: he had been frozen, but now that she had warmed him, he was coming to life again.

In autumn the swallows fly away to foreign lands; but there are some who are late in starting, and then they get so cold that they

"Now You Are to be a Bride!

drop down as if dead, and the snow comes and covers them over.

Thumbelina trembled, she was so frightened; for the bird was very large in comparison with herself – only an inch high. But she took courage, piled the down more closely over the poor swallow, fetched her own coverlet and laid it over his head.

The next night she crept out again to him. There he was alive, but very weak; he could only open his eyes for a moment and look at Thumbelina, who was standing in front of him with a piece of rotten wood in her hand, for she had no other lantern.

"Thank you, pretty little child!" said the swallow to her. "I am so beautifully warm! Soon I shall regain my strength, and then I shall be able to fly out again into the warm sunshine."

"Oh!" she said, "It is very cold outside; it is snowing and freezing! Stay in your warm bed; I will take care of you!"

Then she brought him water in a petal, which he drank, after which he related to her how he had torn one of his wings on a bramble, so that he could not fly as fast as the other swallows, who had flown far away to warmer lands. So at last he had dropped down exhausted, and then he could remember no more.

The whole winter he remained in the tunnel, and Thumbelina looked after him and nursed him tenderly. Neither the mole nor the field-mouse learnt anything of this, for they could not bear the poor swallow.

When the spring came, and the sun warmed the earth again, the swallow said farewell to Thumbelina, who opened the hole in the roof for him which the mole had made. The sun shone brightly down upon her, and the swallow asked her if she would go with him; she could sit upon his back. Thumbelina wanted very much to fly far away into the green wood, but she knew that the old field-mouse would be sad if she ran away. "No, I mustn't come!" she said.

"Farewell, dear good little girl!" said the swallow, and flew off into the sunshine. Thumbelina gazed after him with the tears standing in her eyes, for she was very fond of the swallow.

"Tweet, tweet!" sang the bird, and flew into the green wood. Thumbelina was very unhappy. She was not allowed to go out into the warm sunshine. The corn which had been sowed in the field over the field-mouse's home grew up high into the air, and made a thick forest for the poor little girl, who was only an inch high.

"Now you are to be a bride, Thumbelina!" said the field-mouse, "for our neighbor has proposed to you. What a piece of fortune for a poor child like you! Now you must set to work at your linen for your dowry, for nothing must be lacking if you are to become the wife of our neighbor, the mole!"

Thumbelina had to spin all day long, and every evening the mole visited her, and told her that when the summer was over the sun would not shine so hot; now it was burning the earth as hard as a stone. Yes, when the summer had passed, they would keep the wedding.

But she was not at all pleased about it, for she did not like the mole. Every morning when the sun was rising, and every evening when it was setting, she would steal out of

Goodbye to the Beautiful Sun

the house door, and when the breeze parted the ears of corn so that she could see the blue sky through them, she thought how bright and beautiful it must be outside, and longed to see her dear swallow again. But he never came; no doubt he had flown away far into the great wood.

By the autumn Thumbelina had finished the dowry.

"In four weeks you will be married!" said the field-mouse. "Don't be obstinate, or I shall bite you with my sharp white teeth! You will get a fine husband! The King himself has not such a velvet coat. His store-room and cellar are full, and you should be thankful for that."

Well, the wedding-day arrived. The mole had come to fetch Thumbelina to live with him deep down under the ground, never to come out into the warm sun again, for that was what he didn't like. The poor little girl was very sad, for now she must say goodbye to the beautiful sun.

"Farewell, bright sun!" she cried, stretching out her arms towards it, and taking another step outside the house; for now the corn had been reaped, and only the dry

"Yes, I Will Go With You"

stubble was left standing. "Farewell, farewell!" she said, and put her arms round a little red flower that grew there. "Give my love to the dear swallow when you see him!"

"Tweet, tweet!" sounded in her ear all at once.

She looked up. There was the swallow flying past! As soon as he saw Thumbelina, he was very glad. She told him how unwilling she was to marry the ugly mole, as then she had to live underground where the sun never shone, and she could not help bursting into tears.

"The cold winter is coming now," said the swallow. "I must fly away to warmer lands: will you come with me? You can sit on my back, and we will fly far away from the ugly mole and his dark house, over the mountains, to the warm countries where the sun shines more brightly than here, where it is always summer, and there are always beautiful flowers. Do come with me, dear little Thumbe-lina, who saved my life when I lay frozen in the dark tunnel!"

"Yes, I will go with you," said Thumbelina, and got on the swallow's back, with her feet

A Little Man in the Middle of the Flower

on one of his outstretched wings. Up he flew into the air, over woods and seas, over the great mountains where the snow is always lying. And if she was cold she crept under his warm feathers, only keeping her little head out to admire all the beautiful things in the world beneath.

At last they came to warm lands; there the sun was brighter, the sky seemed twice as high, and in the hedges hung the finest green and purple grapes; in the woods grew oranges and lemons: the air was scented with myrtle and mint, and on the roads were pretty little children running about and playing with great gorgeous butterflies.

But the swallow flew on farther, and it became more and more beautiful. Under the most splendid green trees beside a blue lake stood a glittering white-marble castle. Vines hung about the high pillars; there were many swallows' nests, and in one of these lived the swallow who was carrying Thumbelina.

"Here is my house!" said he. "But it won't do for you to live with me; I am not tidy enough to please you. Find a home for yourself in one of the lovely flowers that grow

A Beautiful Pair of Wings

down there; now I will set you down, and you can do whatever you like."

"That will be splendid!" said she, clapping her little hands.

There lay a great white marble column which had fallen to the ground and broken into three pieces, but between these grew the most beautiful white flowers. The swallow flew down with Thumbelina, and set her upon one of the broad leaves.

But there, to her astonishment, she found a tiny little man sitting in the middle of the flower, as white and transparent as if he were made of glass; he had the prettiest golden crown on his head, and the most beautiful wings on his shoulders; he himself was no bigger than Thumbelina.

He was the spirit of the flower. In each blossom there dwelt a tiny man or woman; but this one was the King over the others.

"How handsome he is!" whispered Thumbelina to the swallow.

The little King was very much frightened at the swallow, for in comparison with one so tiny as himself he seemed a giant. But when he saw Thumbelina, he was delighted, for she was the most beautiful girl he had ever seen. So he took his golden crown from off his head and put it on hers, asking her name, and if she would be his wife, and then she would be Queen of all the flowers.

Yes! He was a different kind of husband than the son of the toad or the mole with the white velvet coat. So she said, "Yes!" to the noble King.

And out of each flower came a lady and gentleman, each so tiny and pretty that it was a pleasure to see them. Each brought Thumbelina a present, but the best of all was a beautiful pair of wings which were fastened on to her back, and now she too could fly from flower to flower.

They all wished her joy, and the swallow sat above in his nest and sang the wedding march, and that he did as well as he could; but he was sad, because he was very fond of Thumbelina and did not want to be separated from her.

"You shall not be called Thumbelina!" said the King to her. "That is an ugly name, and you are much too pretty for that. We will call you May Blossom."

"Farewell, farewell!" said the little swallow with a heavy heart, and flew away to farther lands, far, far away, back north. There he had a little nest above a window, where his wife lived, who can tell fairy stories. "Tweet, tweet!" he sang to her. And that is the way we learnt the whole story.

"If Only We Had!"

PRINCE RABBIT

Once upon a time there was a King who had no children. Sometimes he would say to the Queen, "If only we had a son!" And the Queen would answer, "If only we had!" And then on another day he would say, "If only we had a daughter!" And the Queen would sigh and answer, "Yes, if we had a daughter, that would be something." But they had no children at all.

As the years went on, and there were still no children in the Royal Palace, the people began to ask each other who would be the next King to reign over them. And some said that perhaps it would be the Chancellor, which was a pity, as nobody liked him very much; and others said that there would be no King at all, but that everybody would be equal. Those who were lowest of all thought

"Then I Don't Think Much of It"

that this would be a satisfactory ending of the matter; but those who were higher up felt that, though in some respects it would be a good thing, yet in other respects it would be an ill-advised state of affairs; and they hoped, therefore, that a young Prince would be born in the Palace. But no Prince was born.

One day, when the Chancellor was in audience with the King, it seemed well to him to speak what was in the people's minds.

"Your Majesty," he said and then stopped, wondering how best to put it.

"Well?" said the King.

"Have I your Majesty's permission to speak my mind?"

"So far yes," said the King.

Encouraged by this, the Chancellor resolved to put the matter plainly.

"In the event of your Majesty's death — " He coughed and began again. "If your Majesty ever *should* die," he said, "which in any case will not be for many years — if ever — as, I need hardly say, your Majesty's loyal subjects earnestly hope — I mean they hope

The Chancellor Retired Backwards Out of the Palace

it will be never. But assuming for the moment — making the sad assumption — "

"You said you wanted to speak your mind," interrupted the King. "Is this it?"

"Yes, your Majesty."

"Then I don't think much of it."

"Thank you, your Majesty."

"What you are trying to say is, 'Who will be the next King?' "

"Quite so, your Majesty."

"Ah!" The King was silent for a little. Then he said, "I can tell you who won't be."

The Chancellor did not seek for information on this point, feeling that in the circumstances the answer was obvious.

"What do you suggest yourself?"

"That your Majesty choose a successor from among the young and highly born of the country, putting him to whatever test seems good to your Majesty."

The King pulled at his beard and frowned.

"There must be not one test, but many tests.

There was also One Rabbit

Let all who will offer themselves, provided only that they are under the age of twenty and are well-born. See to it."

He waved his hand in dismissal, and with an accuracy established by long practice the Chancellor retired backwards out of the Palace.

On the following morning, therefore, it was announced that all those who were ambitious to be appointed the King's successor, and who were of high birth and not yet come to the age of twenty, should present themselves a week later for the tests to which His Majesty desired to put them, the first of which was to be a running race. Whereat the people rejoiced, for they wished to be ruled by one to whom they could look up, and running was much esteemed in that country.

On the appointed day the excitement was great. All along the course, which was once round the castle, large crowds were massed, and at the finishing point the King and Queen themselves were seated in a specially erected pavilion. And to this pavilion the competitors were brought to be introduced to their Majesties. And there were nine young nobles, well-built, and handsome, and (it was

Lord Calomel Comes in Second

thought) intelligent, who were competitors. And there was also one Rabbit.

The Chancellor had first noticed the Rabbit when he was lining up the competitors, pinning numbers on their backs so that the people could identify them, and giving them such instructions as seemed necessary to him. "Now, now, be off with you," he had said. "Competitors only, this way." And he had made a motion of impatient dismissal with his foot.

"I *am* a competitor," said the Rabbit. "And I don't think it is usual," he added with dignity, "for the starter to kick one of the competitors just at the beginning of an important foot-race. It looks like favoritism."

"You can't be a competitor," laughed all the young nobles.

"Why not? Read the rules."

The Chancellor, feeling rather hot suddenly, read the rules. The Rabbit was certainly under twenty; he had a pedigree which showed that he was of the highest birth; and –

"And," said the Rabbit, "I am ambitious

to be appointed the King's successor. Those were all the conditions. Now let's get on with the race."

But first came the introduction to the King. One by one the competitors came up... and at the end —

"This," said the Chancellor, as airily as he could, "is Rabbit."

Rabbit bowed in the most graceful manner possible; first to the King and then to the Queen. But the King only stared at him. Then he turned to the Chancellor.

"Well?"

The Chancellor shrugged his shoulders.

"His entry does not appear to lack validity," he said.

"He means, your Majesty, that it is all right," explained Rabbit.

The King laughed suddenly. "Go on," he said. "We can always have a race for a new Chancellor afterwards."

So the race was started. And the young Lord Calomel was much cheered on coming in second; not only by their Majesties, but also by Rabbit, who had finished the course some time before, and was now lounging in the Royal Pavilion.

"A very good style, your Majesty," said Rabbit, turning to the King. "Altogether he seems to be a most promising youth."

"Most," said the King grimly. "So much so that I do not propose to trouble the rest of the competitors. The next test shall take place between you and him."

"Not racing again, please, your Majesty. That would hardly be fair to his lordship."

"No, not racing; fighting."

"Ah! What sort of fighting?"

"With swords," said the King.

"I am a little rusty with swords, but I daresay in a day or two – "

"It will be now," said the King.

"You mean, your Majesty, as soon as Lord Calomel has recovered his breath?"

The King answered nothing, but turned to his Chancellor.

A Short, But Exciting, Struggle

"Tell the young Lord Calomel that in half an hour I desire him to fight with this Rabbit — "

"The young Lord Rabbit," murmured the other competitor to the Chancellor.

"To fight with him for my kingdom."

"*And* borrow me a sword, will you?" said Rabbit. "Quite a small one. I don't want to hurt him."

So, half an hour later, on a level patch of grass in front of the pavilion, the fight began. It was a short, but exciting, struggle. Calomel, whirling his long sword in his strong right arm, dashed upon Rabbit, and Rabbit, carrying his short sword in his teeth, dodged between Calomel's legs and brought him toppling.

And when it was seen that the young Lord rose from the ground with a broken arm, and that with the utmost gallantry he had now taken his sword in his left hand, the people cheered. And Rabbit, dropping his sword for a moment, cheered, too; and then he picked it up and got it entangled in his adversary's legs again, so that again the young Lord Calomel

"The Answer Has Never Been Revealed"

crashed to the ground, this time with a sprained ankle. And there he lay.

Rabbit trotted into the Royal Pavilion, and dropped his sword in the Chancellor's lap.

"Thank you so much," he said. "Have I won?"

The King frowned and pulled at his beard.

"There are other tests," he muttered.

But what were they to be? It was plain that Lord Calomel was in no condition for another physical test. What, then, of an intellectual test?

"After all," said the King to the Queen that night, "intelligence is a quality not without value to a ruler."

"Is it?" asked the Queen doubtfully.

"I have found it so," said the King, a little haughtily.

"Oh," said the Queen.

"There is a riddle, of which my father was fond, the answer to which has never been revealed save to the Royal House. We might make this the final test between them."

"What is the riddle?"

"I fancy it goes like this." He thought for a moment, and then recited it, beating time with his hand.

"My *first* I do for your delight,
Although 'tis neither black nor white.
My *second* looks the other way,
Yet always goes to bed by day.
My *whole* can fly, and climb a tree,
And sometimes swims upon the sea."

"What is the answer?" asked the Queen.

"As far as I remember," said His Majesty, "it is either *Dormouse* or *Raspberry*."

" 'Dormouse' doesn't make sense," objected the Queen.

"Neither does 'raspberry,' " pointed out the King.

"Then how can they guess it?"

"They can't. But my idea is that young Calomel should be secretly told beforehand what the answer is, so that he may win the competition."

"Is that fair?" asked the Queen doubtfully.

"Yes," said the King. "Certainly. Or I wouldn't have suggested it."

So it was duly announced by the Chancellor that the final test between the young Lord Calomel and Rabbit would be the solving of an ancient riddle-me-ree, which in the past had baffled all save those of Royal blood. Copies of the riddle had been sent to the competitors, and in a week from that day they would be called upon to give their answers before their Majesties and the full Court. And with Lord Calomel's copy went a message, which said this:

"*From a Friend.* The answer is *Dormouse.* BURN THIS."

The day came round; and Calomel and Rabbit were brought before their Majesties; and they bowed to their Majesties, and were ordered to be seated, for Calomel's ankle was still painful to him. And when the Chancellor had called for silence, the King addressed those present, explaining the conditions of the test to them.

"And the answer to the riddle," he said,

Rabbit Noticing the Nod

"is in this sealed paper, which I now hand to my Chancellor, in order that he shall open it, as soon as the competitors have told us what they know of the matter."

The people, being uncertain what else to do, cheered slightly.

"I will ask Lord Calomel first," His Majesty went on. He looked at his lordship, and his lordship nodded slightly. And Rabbit, noticing that nod, smiled suddenly to himself.

"Lord Calomel," said the King, "what do you consider to be the best answer to this riddle-me-ree?"

The young Lord Calomel tried to look very wise, and he said:

"There are many possible answers to this riddle-me-ree, but the best answer seems to be *Dormouse.*"

"Let someone take a note of that answer," said the King; whereupon the Chief Secretary wrote down: "LORD CALOMEL – *Dormouse.*"

"Now," said the King to Rabbit, "what suggestion have you to make in this matter?"

Rabbit, who had spent an anxious week

Fifty-four or Forty-two?

inventing answers each more impossible than the last, looked down modestly.

"Well?" said the King.

"Your Majesty," said Rabbit with some apparent hesitation, "I have a great respect for the intelligence of the young Lord Calomel, but I think that in this matter he is mistaken. The answer is not, as he suggests, *wood-louse,* but *dormouse.*"

"I *said* 'dormouse,' " cried Calomel indignantly.

"I thought you said 'wood-louse,' " said Rabbit in surprise.

"He certainly said 'dormouse,' " said the King coldly.

" 'Wood-louse,' I *think,*" said Rabbit.

"Lord Calomel – *'Dormouse,'* " read out the Chief Secretary.

"There you are," said Calomel. "I did say 'dormouse.' "

"My apologies," said Rabbit, with a bow. "Then we are both right, for *dormouse* it certainly is."

"I Declare Lord Calomel the Winner"

The Chancellor broke open the sealed paper, and to the amazement of nearly all present read out *"Dormouse."*

"Apparently, your Majesty," he said in some surprise, "they are both equally correct."

The King scowled. In some way, which he didn't quite understand, he had been tricked.

"May I suggest, your Majesty," the Chancellor went on, "that they be asked now some question of a different order, such as can be answered, after not more than a few minutes' thought, here in your Majesty's presence. Some problem in the higher mathematics, for instance, such as might be profitable for a future King to know."

"What question?" asked His Majesty, a little nervously.

"Well, as an example – what is seven times six?" And, behind his hand, he whispered to the King, "Forty-two."

Not a muscle of the King's face moved, but he looked thoughtfully at the Lord Calomel. Supposing his lordship did not know!

"Well?" he said reluctantly. "What is the answer?"

The young Lord Calomel thought for some time, and then said, "Fifty-four."

"And you?" said the King to Rabbit.

Rabbit wondered what to say. As long as he gave the same answers as Calomel, he could not lose in the encounter, yet in this case "Forty-two" was the right answer. But the King, who could do no wrong, even in arithmetic, might decide, for the purposes of the competition, that "Fifty-four" was an answer more becoming to the future ruler of the country. Was it, then, safe to say "Forty-two?"

"Your Majesty," he said, "there are several possible answers to this extraordinarily novel conundrum. At first sight the obvious solution would appear to be 'Forty-two.' The objection to this solution is that it lacks originality. I have long felt that a progressive country such as ours might well strike out a new line in the matter. Let us agree that in future seven sixes are fifty-four. In that case the answer, as Lord Calomel has pointed out, *is* 'Fifty-four.' But if your Majesty would prefer to cling to the old style of counting, then your Majesty and your Majesty's Chancellor would make the answer 'Forty-two.'"

After saying which, Rabbit bowed gracefully, both to their Majesties and to his opponent, and sat down again.

The King scratched his head in a puzzled sort of way.

"The correct answer," he said, "is, or will be in the future, 'Fifty-four.'"

"Make a note of that," whispered the Chancellor to the Chief Secretary.

"Lord Calomel guessed this at his first attempt; Rabbit at his second attempt. I therefore declare Lord Calomel the winner."

"Shame!" said Rabbit.

"Who said that?" cried the King furiously.

Rabbit looked over his shoulder, with the object of identifying the culprit, but was apparently unsuccessful.

"However," went on the King, "in order that there should be no doubt in the minds of my people as to the absolute fairness with

"I Can Turn a Plum Pudding into a Rabbit"

which this competition is being conducted, there will be one further test. It happens that a King is often called upon to make speeches and exhortations to his people, and for this purpose the ability to stand evenly upon two legs for a considerable length of time is of much value to him. The next test, therefore, will be – "

But at this point Lord Calomel cleared his throat so loudly that the King had to stop and listen to him.

"Quite so," said the King. "The next test, therefore, will be held in a month's time, when his lordship's ankle is healed, and it will be a test to see who can balance himself longest upon two legs only."

Rabbit lolloped back to his home in the wood, pondering deeply.

Now there was an enchanter who lived in the wood, a man of many magical gifts. He could (it was averred by the countryside) extract colored ribbons from his mouth, cook plum-puddings in a hat, and produce as many as ten silk handkerchiefs, knotted together, from a twist of paper. And that night, after a

"I am Lord Calomel"

simple dinner of salad, Rabbit called upon him.

"Can you," he said, "turn a rabbit into a man?"

The enchanter considered this carefully.

"I can," he said at last, "turn a plum-pudding into a rabbit."

"That," said Rabbit, "to be quite frank, would not be a helpful operation."

"I can turn almost anything into a rabbit," said the enchanter with growing enthusiasm. "In fact, I like doing it."

Then Rabbit had an idea.

"Can you turn a man into a rabbit?"

"I did once. At least I turned a baby into a baby rabbit."

"When was that?"

"Eighteen years ago. At the court of King Nicodemus. I was giving an exhibition of my powers to him and his good Queen. I asked one of the company to lend me a baby, never thinking for a moment that – the young Prince was handed up. I put a red silk

"Son of the Late King Nicodemus"

handkerchief over him, and waved my hands. Then I took the handkerchief away.... The Queen was very much distressed. I tried everything I could, but it was useless. The King was most generous about it. He said that I could keep the rabbit. I carried it about with me for some weeks, but one day it escaped. Dear, dear!" He wiped his eyes gently with a red silk handkerchief.

"Most interesting," said Rabbit. "Well, this is what I want you to do." And they discussed the matter from the beginning.

A month later the great Standing Competition was to take place. When all was ready, the King rose to make his opening remarks.

"We are now," he began, "to make one of the most interesting tests between our two candidates for the throne. At the word 'Go!' they will — " And then he stopped suddenly. "Why, what's this?" he said, putting on his spectacles. "Where is the young Lord Calomel? And what is that second rabbit doing? There was no need to bring your brother," he added severely to Rabbit.

"I am Lord Calomel," said the second rabbit meekly.

"Oh!" said the King.

"Go!" said the Chancellor, who was a little deaf.

Rabbit, who had been practising for a month, jumped on his back paws and remained there. Lord Calomel, who had no practice at all, remained on all fours. In the crowd at the back the enchanter chuckled to himself.

"How long do I stay like this?" asked Rabbit.

"This is all very awkward and distressing," said the King.

"May I get down?" said Rabbit.

"There is no doubt that the Rabbit has won," said the Chancellor.

"Which rabbit?" cried the King crossly. "They're both rabbits."

"The one with the white spots behind the ears," said Rabbit helpfully. "May I get down?"

There was a sudden cry from the back of the hall.

"Your Majesty!"

"Well, well, what is it?"

The enchanter pushed his way forward.

"May I look, your Majesty?" he said in a trembling voice. "White spots behind the ears? Dear, dear! Allow me!" He seized Rabbit's ears, and bent them this way and that.

"Ow!" said Rabbit.

"It is! Your Majesty, it is!"

"Is what?"

"The son of the late King Nicodemus, whose country is now joined to your own. Prince Silvio."

"Quite so," said Rabbit airily, hiding his surprise. "Didn't any of you recognize me?"

"Nicodemus only had one son," said the Chancellor, "and he died as a baby."

"Not died," said the enchanter, and forthwith explained the whole sad story.

"I see," said the King, when the story was ended. "But of course that is neither here nor

"Hey Presto!"

there. A competition like this must be conducted with absolute impartiality." He turned to the Chancellor. "Which of them won that last test?"

"Prince Silvio," said the Chancellor.

"Then, my dear Prince Silvio –

"One moment," interrupted the enchanter excitedly. "I've just thought of the words. I *knew* there were some words you had to say."

He threw his red silk handkerchief over Rabbit, and cried, "Hey presto! And the handkerchief rose and rose and rose.. . . And there was Prince Silvio!

You can imagine how loudly the people cheered. But the King appeared not to notice that anything surprising had happened.

"Then, my dear Prince Silvio," he went on, "as the winner of this most interesting series of contests, you are appointed successor to our throne."

"Your Majesty," said Silvio, "this is too much." And he turned to the enchanter and said, "May I borrow your handkerchief for a moment? My emotion has overcome me."

So on the following day, Prince Rabbit was duly proclaimed heir to the throne before all

The King Gave a Great Party

the people. But not until the ceremony was over did he return the enchanter's red handkerchief.

"And now," he said to the enchanter, "you may restore Lord Calomel to his proper shape."

And the enchanter placed his handkerchief on Lord Calomel's head, and said "Hey presto!" and Lord Calomel stretched himself and said, "Thanks very much." But he said it rather coldly, as if he were not really very grateful.

So they all lived happily for a long time. And Prince Rabbit married the most beautiful Princess of those parts; and when a son was born to them there was much feasting and jollification. And the King gave a great party, whereat minstrels, tumblers, jugglers and such like were present in large quantities to give pleasure to the company. But in spite of a suggestion made by the Princess, the enchanter was not present.

"But I hear he is so clever," said the Princess to her husband.

"He has many amusing inventions," replied the Prince, "but some of them are not in the best of taste."

"Very well, dear," said the Princess.

TITLES AVAILABLE IN THIS SERIES